The BOY with BIG, BIG FEELINGS

by

BRITNEY WINN LEE

Illustrated by

JACOB SOUVA

beaming books
MINNEAPOLIS

31 30 29 28 27 26 16 17 18 19 20 21 22

Print ISBN: 978-1-5064-5450-4
eBook ISBN: 978-1-5064-8022-0

Names: Lee, Britney Winn, author. | Souva, Jacob, illustrator.
Title: The boy with big, big feelings / written by Britney Winn Lee ;
illustrated by Jacob Souva.
Description: Minneapolis, MN : Beaming Books, 2019. | Summary: "Meet a boy with a heart so big, his feelings glow from his cheeks, spill out of his eyes, and jump up and down on his chest. What good is this giant heart?"--Provided by publisher.
Identifiers: LCCN 2019003872 | ISBN 9781506454504 (hardcover : alk. paper)
Subjects: | CYAC: Stories in rhyme. | Emotions--Fiction. | Empathy--Fiction.
Classification: LCC PZ8.3.L49918 Boy 2019 | DDC [E]--dc23
LC record available at https://lccn.loc.gov/2019003872

Beaming Books
PO Box 1209
Minneapolis, MN 55440-1209
Beamingbooks.com

Printed in China

To Luke, with your big heart, for cultivating the big heart of our boy. Deeply, daily.

—B.W.L.

There once was a boy with feathery hair
and a heart that was bursting with feeling.
His emotions seemed bigger than everyone else's,
and sometimes they made him go reeling.

When playing outside on the yellowest days,

a loud truck might rumble on by.

And wouldn't you know it, that big heart of his

would push feelings right out of his eyes!

At night when the shadows would form on the walls

and fear would steal all of his rest,

those feelings of his made it so hard to breathe

as they jumped up and down on his chest.

Sometimes when his play had to come to an end

or when things didn't go as he'd planned,

the feelings would run down the length of his arms

and clench when they got to his hands.

He felt happy feelings as big as the others
from tickles and hide-and-go-seek
and jokes and races and stories and songs
that made feelings glow from his cheeks.

9.c
b
Fig.10.
9.f
9.d

Beautiful things would stick in his brain

and not leave him for hours and hours:

the fur of a dog, a fluffy white cloud,

his mama, a banjo, some flowers.

But when someone he loved had a very hard day,

he'd feel he'd been over-equipped

to feel all their feelings as deeply as they,

which would quiver right out of his lip.

He wondered, “Why me? Why this big, giant heart
in a world that’s so heavy and kind,
where all of the feelings under the sun
feel as if they were made to be mine?”

HOOLS

So the boy tried to stuff all his feelings deep down,

to control what he thought he should hide,

afraid that the others would make fun of him

if they saw all he felt deep inside.

Would they think he was weak? Dramatic? Afraid?

Would they call him a wimp or a baby?

If they saw the big, thumping heart in his chest,

would they not want to play with him, maybe?

A
B
C
D
Welc

But while swinging one day, feeling oh so alone,

he noticed a girl feeling blue.

He marveled: What's that? Could it be? Yes, indeed!

Her emotions were extra big, too!

"Are you okay?" the boy asked the girl.

"I'm fine. Just, sometimes I get sad."

He said, “You do? Hey, I get sad, too!

I get scared and silly and mad!”

4-0
5-0

The two became pals who shared their big hearts,
not feeling they had to pretend
when they needed to cry or to laugh big and loud,
since feelings had helped make them friends!

And soon, they noticed there were other big hearts

in the classroom, the playground, the bus,

and they smiled as they learned that it wasn't just them.

"Big emotions affect ALL of us!"

The boy and his friends slowly felt less alone
with the feelings that lived deep inside them.
Emotions might feel big and scary sometimes,
but that is no reason to hide them!

BRITNEY WINN LEE is an author, editor, and nonprofit director living in Shreveport, Louisiana, with her creative husband and big-hearted son. She serves as the full-time director of Noel Community Arts Program and the part-time editor and content coordinator for Red Letter Christians. With a BA in religious studies and a master's degree in nonprofit administration, Britney has worked for over a decade in faith- and justice-based creative community-building.

JACOB SOUVA is an illustrator who lives in Upstate New York with his wife and two boys. He's passionate about equipping kids with language to navigate their emotional well-being, laugh at silly things, and be inspired by big stories. Jacob works digitally and loves to experiment with texture and color.